The Mouse Wedding

Retold by
Mairi Mackinnon

Illustrated by
Frank Endersby

Reading Consultant: Alison Kelly
Roehampton University

This story is about

Father
Mouse,

Mother
Mouse,
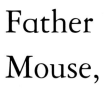

Miss
Mouse,

USBORNE FIRST READING

should be re_ned to any bran_'
ounty Libra _n _ befor_

USBORNE FIRST
The
Gingerbread
Man

retold by
Mairi Mackinnon
Illustrated by Elena Temporin

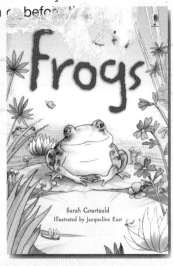

Frogs

Sarah Courtauld
Illustrated by Jacqueline East

USBORNE FIRST READING

The Goose
that laid the
Golden Eggs

based on the fable by
Aesop

Illustrated by
Daniel Howarth

USBORNE FIRST READING

The
ENORMOUS
TURNIP

based on the story by Alexei Tolstoy
Illustrated by Georgien Overwater

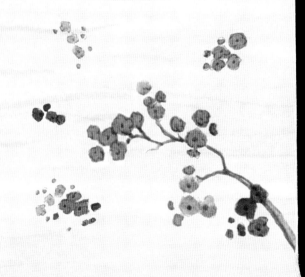

the sun,   a cloud,

the wind,   a wall

and a handsome
young mouse.

Once there was a family
of mice – Father Mouse,

Mother Mouse and little
Miss Mouse.

And then one day
Miss Mouse wasn't so
little anymore.

"Goodness me!" said
Father Mouse. "It's time
you got married."

"Pack your bag," he said.
"We're going on a journey."

"We must find you the
best, most powerful
husband in the world!"

"Who could that be?"
asked Miss Mouse.

Father Mouse thought
for a moment. "The sun!"
he said.

"He makes our days bright and warm, and helps the flowers grow. Let's ask him."

The mouse family
climbed a high mountain.

They waited until
evening, when the sun
was low in the sky.

"Oh Mr. Sun," said Father Mouse. "You are more powerful than anyone else in the world..."

...aren't you?

"Powerful? Me?" said
the sun. "Oh no, I don't
think so."

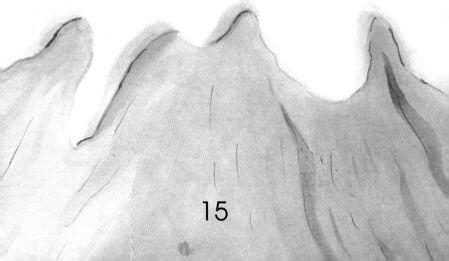

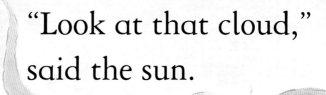

"Look at that cloud," said the sun.

"He can cover my face, and block all my light and warmth. There's nothing I can do."

"Well, then, we must talk to the cloud," said Father Mouse.

The mouse family went
a little way down the
mountain and slept until
morning.

When they woke up, there
was the cloud resting on
the mountain top.

"Oh Mr. Cloud," said Father Mouse. "You are more powerful than anyone else in the world..."

...aren't you?

"Powerful? Me?" said the cloud. "Oh no, I don't think so."

"Wait until the wind blows," said the cloud.

"He can push me around, this way and that way. There's nothing I can do."

"Well, then, we must talk to the wind," said Father Mouse.

Mother Mouse gave
everyone some crumbs for
breakfast, and the mice
waited.

The wind soon rose and
blew the cloud away.

"Oh Mr. Wind," said
Father Mouse. "You are
more powerful than
anyone else in the world..."

...aren't you?

"Powerful? Me?" said the wind. "Oh no, I don't think so."

"Up here
I can blow
where I like,"
said the wind.
"But when I meet a wall,
there's nothing I can do."

"Well, then, we must talk to a wall," said Father Mouse.

Talk to a wall?

The mouse family set off
down the mountain.

After a while, they came to
a high wall.

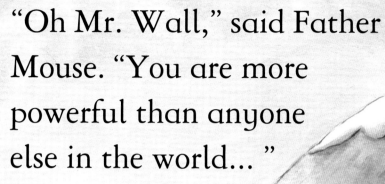

"Oh Mr. Wall," said Father Mouse. "You are more powerful than anyone else in the world... "

...aren't you?

"Powerful? Me?" said
the wall. "Oh no, I don't
think so."

"I may look strong and
tall," said the wall, "but
I can feel a little mouse,
nibbling me to dust.
There's nothing I can do."

"Well, then, we must
talk to the mouse," said
Father Mouse.

"Oh yes, please let's talk to the mouse," said Miss Mouse.

They made their way
along the wall. There
was a mousehole and a
handsome young mouse.

Miss Mouse smiled at him.

"Oh Mr. Mouse," said Father Mouse. "You are more powerful than anyone else in the world... aren't you?"

"Well..." the mouse began.
"You're more powerful
than the wall," said Miss
Mouse quickly.

"...who is more powerful than the wind," added Mother Mouse.

"...who is more powerful than the cloud," said Father Mouse.

"...who is more powerful than the sun!" finished Miss Mouse.

"Oh," said the handsome
young mouse. "Then I
suppose I am."

"In that case," said Father Mouse, "will you marry my daughter?"

"I'd love to!" said the handsome young mouse.

So the mice were married
next to the wall.

The sun and the cloud and
the wind all came to the
wedding...

But not all at once.

Designed by Emily Bornoff
Series designer: Russell Punter
Series editor: Lesley Sims

First published in 2008 by Usborne Publishing Ltd., Usborne House,
83-85 Saffron Hill, London EC1N 8RT, England. www.usborne.com
Copyright © 2008 Usborne Publishing Ltd.

48

USBORNE FIRST READING
Level Four

USBORNE FIRST READING
The Dragon Painter

retold by
Rosie Dickins
Illustrated by John Nez

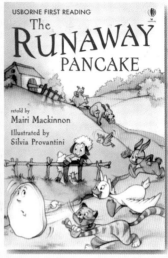

USBORNE FIRST READING
The RUNAWAY PANCAKE

retold by
Mairi Mackinnon
Illustrated by
Silvia Provantini

USBORNE FIRST READING
Little Red Riding Hood

based on the story by The Brothers Grimm
Illustrated by Mike Gordon

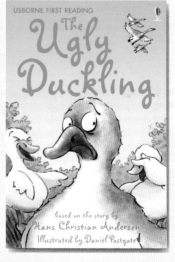

USBORNE FIRST READING
The Ugly Duckling

based on the story by
Hans Christian Andersen
Illustrated by Daniel Postgate